A PROMISE OF LOVE

J.M. GOODRICH

A Promise Of Love

J.M. Goodrich

After a whirlwind romance on a sun-soaked island, Ally and Darren return to the city, determined to turn their vacation love into something real. But as Darren struggles to adjust to the fast-paced urban life, Ally can't help but worry as he confesses his nostalgia for the island. Their relationship faces its biggest test when Darren's ex unexpectedly appears at their best friend's wedding, intent on rekindling old flames. Ally is torn, fearing she might lose Darren to both his past love and the life he left behind. Will their love be strong enough to weather the storm?

CHAPTER 1

lly

WALKING OFF THE PLANE, I have never felt more nervous. It was impulsive enough for me to have just flown out for the unplanned vacation I was returning from. But now I was returning with a man.

A man that I had just met.

A man that I was falling in love with.

But that's not what I was so nervous about. I was more afraid of what my friends would think about all of this.

This all was very unlike me. I didn't do things like this.

At all.

I was one who lived quietly, obeying all rules and staying out of everyone's way. I never caused any trouble, that just wasn't who I was.

And now this.

I must be completely out of my mind.

But . . . you only live once, as the saying goes. And I want to live as happily as I can.

This trip did much more than rejuvenate my mind and give me a nice tan.

It showed me that it's okay to just let go and live a little. It showed me that it's perfectly okay to slow down and truly enjoy the little things.

And I intend to do just that.

I looked at Darren, standing next to me as we waited to retrieve our luggage. I still can't believe he agreed to come with me. "I told you I live with a roommate, right?" I asked him nervously.

He smiled, grabbing my hand reassuringly. "You did. And I promise I'll be on my absolute best behavior. I'll even stay in a hotel if they don't feel comfortable with me there."

I squeezed his hand. I really didn't want him to stay in a hotel. I wanted him to stay by my side.

I never wanted to be away from this man ever again. This was a new feeling for me. But, I suppose it really wasn't up to me though. I didn't live in that apartment alone.

Although I really wish I did right now.

I loved living with Steph. It's been just the two of us for a long time now. Bringing men home wasn't anything new. Well, for Steph, anyways. I never met anyone, not that I was really trying. And that's not to say that she's out with a new guy every night.

She would occasionally bring home a guy. Which was no big deal. I didn't mind. Steph was an adult. And an incredibly responsible one at that.

I trusted her with my life.

Again, I never really did anything like this. So I had no way to prepare myself for what my friends' reactions were going to be.

I really should have warned her. I got so caught up in everything that I never had a chance to tell her the truth. In fact, it never even crossed my mind.

Horrible, I know. I've been incredibly selfish.

Let's just hope she'd be okay with all of this.

We finally located our bags and grabbed them off the conveyor. Hand in hand, we turned and began to walk out of the airport.

"Ready?" I asked Darren, half joking.

"More than you know," he smiled brightly.

"Ally!" I heard someone scream my name. I whipped my head around to see Stephanie and Lily, jumping up and down while waving their arms in my direction like a couple of maniacs.

I felt my face instantly turning red. I had no idea that they were going to be here. I really appreciate the fact that they both came all the way out here to pick me up. I just wish I had more time to prepare everyone.

As Darren and I walked towards my two crazy friends, I could see the surprised and confused looks on their faces as their eyes drifted down to our clasped hands. It made me want to let go of his hand, but I didn't, thinking it might make me feel bad.

Darren had given up so much to be here with me, even if just for a few weeks, so I felt that I owed him a lot. I wanted to avoid making him feel uncomfortable or hurt at all. And I certainly didn't want him to regret his decision to be with me.

Stephanie, regaining her composure, yelled my name again. She began to run through the crowd towards us, with Lily closely following.

I was almost thrown to the ground by the force of my two friends throwing themselves on me in a hug.

"Sorry," I mouthed to Darren, who just took a step back and laughed to himself.

"I missed you guys so much," I told them, squeezing both girls in a hug.

"You have no idea, girl," Stephanie whispered.

Her response made tears well up in my eyes.

Once we all finally untangled ourselves from each other I stood back, ready to introduce Darren to them.

Smiling sweetly at him, I took my place next to him. "These two are my best friends," I told him, waving my hand in their direction. "Stephanie is my roommate, and Lily is the one getting married. Although, she's at our apartment enough that she could be considered a roommate," I laughed.

Which was true, Lily was practically at our place every-day. Which we didn't mind. We loved her company. And I wouldn't have it any other way.

I took a deep breath. "Steph, Lily, this is Darren," I said, nervousness beginning to creep back in. While on vacation I had told Steph that I had met a guy, but that was pretty much it. I hadn't given her any further details. And I had neglected to mention the fact that I would be bringing him home with me.

All that Lily had been told was that I had met a guy and that he would be my date to her wedding. That was it.

And I hadn't even told her about any of this myself, either. I had told her about it in the voicemail I had left her as I was boarding the plane to come home.

Damn, I hadn't really thought anything through, had I?

But Darren simply smiled, his million dollar rock star smile that had melted my heart back on the island. He shook both their hands. "I feel as though I already know the two of you," he said, letting out a small laugh. "Ally talked about the two of you all the time."

I felt my face grow hot.

"From what I've been told, the two of you are the most important people in her life."

"Well, I would hope so," Steph said, flipping her hair over her shoulder. The three of us burst out in laughter.

Seriously, I loved these two.

And their opinion meant the world to me. I wanted them to like Darren.

I needed them to.

And luckily, that seemed to be the case. Which eased my nerves a bit, and I finally began to relax. Steph even looped her arm through his as we all walked out of the airport.

Arriving back home was a different story. Our apartment had only two bedrooms. One being mine and the other one was Steph's. Meaning Darren would have to stay with me.

In my room.

I know we're all adults and this shouldn't be such a big deal. But to me, it was. Darren and I had spent a lot of time together on the island, but we never spent the night together.

And now, the first time that it would be happening, was with my best friend in the room right next to us.

I just really hoped this wouldn't ruin things for us.

Darren and I hadn't been together all that long, I'm not afraid to admit that. But the sparks between us, the connection - it was stronger than anything I've ever felt. It was undeniable. And I would do anything to explore our relationship and see exactly what it could be.

There was no way I couldn't.

I needed to prove to myself that this wasn't just a fling or a short summer romance. This was more. Much more. I felt it in every part of me.

Darren meant more to me than anything.

I watched him as he walked around our small apartment,

checking everything out. It was pretty much the complete opposite of the small house that he had lived in on the island.

There, he had lived in a house with open-air rooms, the ocean breeze filtering in throughout the entire place. It was spacious and illuminated by natural light. Easy to move around in and quiet, with most of the sounds coming from either his guitar playing or the ocean waves.

It was peaceful.

It was calm.

It was magic.

Here . . .

It was loud.

It was chaotic.

It was cramped and stuffy.

But it was home. I was afraid of how hard it might be for Darren to adjust.

After giving him the tour, which took all of thirty seconds, he went to my room to take a short nap.

I guess it was our room for now. The thought brought a smile to my face and some unexpected feelings. As well as some naughty thoughts.

Stephanie went into the kitchen, grabbing a bottle of wine and three glasses. The three of us then took a seat on the couch. The girls scooted over to each side of the couch so that I would be sitting in the middle of them.

"So," Lily said, handing me a glass, "how was your trip?" The look on her face made me grow red again.

"It was good," I said, taking a sip of wine.

Steph looked over at my closed bedroom door and then back at me. "I'd say it was little more than good," she raised her eyebrow at me, lips curled in a smirk.

I blushed deeply, my face mirroring the color of the wine in my glass.

"So . . . tell us," Steph wriggled her eyebrows, making me laugh.

Lily chimed in. "Yeah, we need details, girl. You can't bring a hot guy home to stay and not tell us everything."

Steph and I shot her a look.

"What? I may be engaged, but I am not dead."

I laughed, shaking my head. Darren *was* hot, there was no denying that. I remember the way all those girls looked at him as soon as he stepped on stage.

We sipped on our wine as I told them all about my island adventures.

"I still can't believe you did all this. This is so unlike you, Ally. But girl, you happy," Steph squealed.

"You do," Lily nodded in agreement. "It's about time you found yourself a man," she said as she squished me in a one-armed side hug.

"I am very happy," I admitted. "And," I turned to Steph, " are you absolutely, one hundred percent sure you don't mind me bringing him here to stay for a bit? I feel so bad that I didn't give you a warning."

She waved me off, getting up to place her empty glass in the sink. "Girl, of course I'm okay with it. Besides, how many men have I brought home?" She giggled.

True. It wasn't as if she was bringing home a different guy every night. But she did have her fair share of visitors. She was an adult, and deserved to have her fun.

"Besides," she continued, "the other day I purchased these amazing noise canceling headphones for the times when I work from home. They will also come in handy so I won't have to hear the two of you doing it."

She and Lily erupted into a fit of laughter. I only grew more embarrassed.

My eyes slid to my bedroom door.

Where Darren was asleep.

In my bed.

If you would have asked me just a few weeks ago if I ever imagined this would happen, I would have laughed in your face.

I never imagined that I would go on a spur of the moment trip, resulting in me falling desperately in love.

CHAPTER 2

arren

LIVING with Ally has been amazing so far. Also a little challenging, but amazing. I love everything about this woman. From the moment I first laid eyes on her from the stage at one of my beach gigs, I knew there was something special about her.

I have seen countless women at our shows, many drunk and throwing themselves at me. Screaming and waving their arms around wildly, trying to get my attention.

But Ally was different. It wasn't hard to notice her, alone in a sea of couples. Though she was alone, I didn't get the sense that she was lonely.

She was just sitting at her table, swaying along to the music with a gorgeous smile on her face. She had an air of innocence about her and I knew I just had to get to know her.

I remember walking up to her after that particular show to introduce myself. I've never been so nervous before, about anything in my life. I could play shows in front of hundreds of people with no problem.

But this . . .

The thought of speaking to this one single woman had my nerves all over the place.

But I'm glad I sucked it up and went for it.

I've never been happier.

As much as I love Ally though, living in the city is sometimes a challenge.

I was used to waking up naturally to the sounds of the waves on the shore, sunlight filling the house with its warmth. I loved my slow, lazy mornings. Waking up and having coffee on the beach. Practicing guitar for hours until I either had a gig or had to head to Fred's to help him out a bit.

I missed Fred. And his food. I searched all over but there wasn't any restaurant near here that even came close to Fred's cooking. I called him every day, but it was hard not being able to just walk down the beach to see him.

It was different walking down busy sidewalks instead of sandy beaches, living in a much smaller space with two people instead of alone in my own home. It was sometimes difficult to sleep at night with all the noise from the traffic, but still. I'd endure it all just to be near Ally. I couldn't lose her, no matter what.

While she was at work, I decided to take a walk around the city. It was a beautiful day, the weather perfect, and I didn't feel like staying in the apartment. So I strapped my guitar to my back and headed out the door.

I wandered around, and after a while grabbed lunch at a small cafe in the park. Sitting on a bench while eating my sandwich was nice, but I missed the peacefulness of the beach. I quickly shook the thought out of my head, reminding myself of why I was here.

As I ate, I brought out my guitar, strumming absentmindedly between bites. A few people commented on my playing as they strolled by me on their way through the park. It brought back memories of my normal lunch gigs on the beach back home. Playing in a nearly empty park while seated on a bench instead of standing tall on a stage was an entirely different experience.

With a sigh, I finished my lunch, standing up to throw away my wrappers and empty cup in the garbage bin nearby. As I approached the bench again something caught my ear. A faint, melodious guitar tune drifting through the air. My curiosity was piqued, so I grabbed my guitar and began following the sound through the winding pathways along the park. After a few minutes I came to a small clearing near the center of the park.

Beneath the shade of a huge oak tree stood a man, a little older than myself, playing a guitar with a soulful expression on his face. Surrounding him was a small yet captivated audience, swaying along to the music. I leaned against a nearby tree, listening as well.

The man finished his song with a flourish, and the small crowd went wild. As the cheers died down the man's gaze caught my own. His eyes drifted to my back, lingering on my guitar resting there. He caught my eye once more. This time with a smile and a slight nod.

A silent invitation.

Nodding back I pushed off my tree, walking through the crowd, joining him at his side. "Mind if I join you?" I asked, already knowing the answer.

"Not at all," the man replied. A smile spread across his face, and I took a seat next to him in the grass.

I settled in, my fingers finding familiar chords. Together,

me and my new friend played on, letting our guitars converse, weaving melodies that danced through the leaves and mingled with the crowd, which was slowly growing in size as we played.

I allowed myself to get lost in the music, feeling more at home than I have in days.

CHAPTER 3

lly

LILY HAD DROPPED by for dinner with the three of us, which seemed to be the norm lately. Not that I'm complaining one bit. I love my best friends more than anything, and I love having the chance to be able to get together just about every single day.

I helped Stephanie finish up with the cooking as Darren set the table. It warmed my heart how well he was fitting in here.

"I see I'm just in time," Lily laughed, coming in the door just as I was taking the lasagna out of the oven. "Smells like heaven."

Stephanie beamed at her remark. Lately she had been experimenting in the kitchen, and she had quickly become quite the chef. I'm so proud of her. She made us homemade dinner every night, loving every bit of it. She was also proud of every dish she made.

We set the dishes on the table and all took our seats, digging in.

"How's the wedding planning coming along?" I asked Lily.

She swallowed her bite of salad, eyes lighting up. Lately, her wedding has been her absolute favorite topic. "I'm probably going to jinx myself, but so far everything's going perfectly. I'm so excited, I just wish Stephen wouldn't have to work so much," she pouted.

Stephen, Lily's fiancee, was working at a top law firm. He was currently putting in many hours of overtime so that he and Lily could take off on their month-long honeymoon.

I am *not* jealous of that. At all.

While Lily excitedly talked about her wedding plans and the details, I noticed Darren not really paying attention. I mean, men normally didn't get all excited about wedding planning, but still. Something about this felt different. The look on his face told me something was wrong.

He was sitting there, barely eating anything, as he moved the food around on his plate. He was staring out the window, seeming lost in thoughts. Lily had also noticed. She leaned over and playfully nudged him. "Hey Darren, staring off into space?" She laughed. "Missing those island sunsets?"

Darren chucked weakly. He glanced at me briefly before replying. "A little," he admitted. "Life here is . . . different."

My heart stuttered. I exchanged a quick yet concerned look with Stephanie. I wanted to ask Darren what he meant by that, but chose not to press him in front of everyone. The last thing I wanted to do was embarrass him or to put him on the spot.

We finished eating, Darren trying harder to participate in the conversation. But I could tell something was still bothering him. Stephanie went to the kitchen, coming back with her latest creation, a decadent chocolate pie, for dessert.

Seriously, this pie was dangerous. I could eat it everyday. And not just for dessert.

After helping clear the table, I caught Darren's eye. "Do you want to take a walk?" I whispered. He nodded gratefully.

"Dinner was absolutely delicious, as ever," Darren told Stephanie. She smiled widely at him.

"It was," I agreed. "But if it's okay with you two," I looked to both her and Lily, "Darren and I are going to take a short walk. It's such a gorgeous night."

Steph looked at me worryingly, but I shot her a reassuring look. "Of course," she smiled. "Have a great walk."

We left the apartment, stepping out into the cool evening air. The streets were quiet as we strolled to the park nearby. The roar of the city's hustle and bustle turned to a distant hum. My entire body buzzed with nervousness as I struggled with what to say to Darren.

Finally, he spoke, his voice edged with vulnerability. "Ally, I've been struggling a little," he began, his hands shoved deep into his pockets. "Since leaving the island, everything just sometimes feels a little overwhelming. I miss the simplicity, the peace. I miss Fred." He looked at me earnestly, his eyes searching mine for understanding. "But I love you, Ally. More than anything. I want us to work, no matter what. You are the only thing that's important to me."

My heart ached for him. This is exactly what I've feared since he moved here. I didn't want to lose him, but I didn't want to make him comfortable or come to resent me either. I reached out, grabbing his hands. "I understand. It's a big change, leaving Paradise for this cramped city life. But we're a team," I reassured him. "We'll figure this out together. I'll be here for you, no matter what you need."

Darren's eyes shined, hinting at unshed tears. He pulled me close, wrapping his arms around me. "Thank you," he murmured, pressing a kiss to the top of my head. "You have no idea how much that means to me. And I want you to know that even though I may occasionally have feelings like this, I don't regret moving here to be with you. Not even a little. You are more than worth it."

I squeezed him tighter, my heart full of love and determination. "We'll take it one step at a time. Together. You'll never have to do anything alone."

After holding each other for a bit more, we continued our walk, hand in hand, hearts feeling lighter.

We eventually returned to the apartment, where Steph and Lily were waiting for us. The evening continued with stories and laughter. The air feeling freer.

CHAPTER 4

lly

WHILE LILY WAS out for the day Steph and I snuck into her house, with the help of Stephen, to set everything up for the surprise bridal shower we were throwing for her. Stephen had slipped us a spare key about a week back and was keeping her occupied while we decorated their apartment.

I looked around the room in satisfaction at the scene we had created. Lily's living room had been transformed into a sea of reds and corals, perfectly matching her wedding theme.

Steph finished setting up the mini buffet table just as our guests began to arrive.

Shortly after the last person was through the door, Stephen texted saying they were on their way home. "It's showtime," I announced, slipping my phone into my pocket. We all stood in the center of the room with confetti cannons, nervously awaiting her arrival.

"Surprise!" We all yelled, covering her and Stephen in a shower of confetti.

"You guys," she said, eyes wide and shining with unshed tears. "You didn't have to do this."

"Of course we did," Steph told her as we ran up to hug our friend.

The bridal shower went off without a hitch, and everyone was having a great time. Lily took a sip of her sparkling lemonade and then cleared her throat.

"First of all, I want to thank my two very best friends," she looked to me and Steph, "for throwing me this awesome shower. You two are amazing."

We raised our glasses. "Anything for you, girl."

"And second," she continued, "I know this has nothing to do with today, but it is a great day. And I have some great news. And since you are all here, I'd like to share it with you." She paused for a second. My eyes clicked to her stomach, thinking this was a pregnancy announcement. "I got a promotion at work!" She beamed with excitement. Everyone cheered for her.

I, on the other hand, had mixed emotions. Which instantly had me feeling guilty. Of course I was happy for my friend. She had been working for this for years. It was a huge promotion. A huge opportunity for her.

But at the same time, I couldn't help but be a little sad. And maybe a bit jealous.

I was again passed up for yet another deserved promotion at my own job.

But still, I put on a smile for my best friend. Today was not at all about me.

"Oh, my gosh," Emma added. "That's amazing Lily. Congratulations! Not to step on your achievements, but I also got promoted at my work too!"

"Oh wow!" Lily told our friend. "I'm so happy for you!"

Everyone smiled and clapped, while the two excitedly hugged each other. The focus of the evening quickly turned to everyone and their own accomplishments.

I smiled along and congratulated everyone, but otherwise kept to myself. With everyone talking about all the new and exciting things happening in their lives as well as Darren's recent confession of missing home . . . I was a complete mess inside. I had a constant storm of emotions swirling around.

But I was determined not to show it.

"Are you okay, Ally?" Lily's concerned voice interrupted my thoughts.

I forced a smile. "Of course, everything's great," I lied, beginning to clean up as the evening came to a close."I'm just so happy for you, Lily. You have so many great things going for you."

Lily sighed happily. "Life is pretty amazing right now."

"It sure is," I pulled her in for a hug.

Lily, observant as she is, placed her hands on my shoulders. "But really, what is going on with you?"

I sighed heavily, not wanting to bring down the mood on her special day.

"You know you can tell me anything," she continued. "Nothing you have to say will ruin the atmosphere," she reassured, as if reading my mind.

"It's Darren," I finally said, and Lily raised an eyebrow in concern.

"Everything alright with you two?"

"Yes, although he recently admitted the fact that he misses life on the island sometimes."

"Oh, well that's to be expected. City life and island life are completely different. I wouldn't think it would be easy for anyone."

"True," I said. But then an idea hit me, and excitement ran through me. "Can I run something by you?"

"Sure," Lily said. "What's up?"

I took a deep breath, excitedly launching into my idea.

CHAPTER 5

arren

I COULDN'T STOP STARING at Ally. She looked absolutely radiant in her coral colored bridesmaid dress. It was a gorgeous off the shoulder, floor length chiffon dress. It had a thigh high slit in the left. With her flowing brown hair done up in beach waves, she looked like a dream.

We finished getting ready for the wedding and headed to the venue a little early. Ally wanted to help check everything out and make sure it would be absolutely perfect for her best friend's big day.

While Ally was off checking flower arrangements and chair placemats, I spotted Stephen and wandered over to him.

"How are you holding up?" I asked, clasping his hand and patting him on the back.

"A little nervous, not gonna lie," he laughed. "But I've also never felt more ready for anything in my entire life. I knew that I was going to marry Lily the first moment I ever laid eyes on her."

I nodded, knowing exactly what he meant. I felt the same way about Ally.

I'm nowhere near ready for marriage. Not yet. But I do know without a doubt that she is the one I'm going to spend the rest of my life with.

I've had girlfriends before, but never have I felt anything quite this deep. I couldn't imagine my life without Ally.

I looked over at her, fussing with a bouquet of flowers. She looked like a goddess as the sun hit her just right.

She simply took my breath away.

I watched as she suddenly took out her phone, checking her messages. Her eyes lit up as she read whatever was on the screen. As she was putting her phone away her eyes searched the venue, stopping once she spotted me.

In an instant she rushed over to me, the most excited look on her face.

"I'm sorry, but can I borrow Darren for a minute?" She asked Stephen.

"Of course," he said. "I need a drink anyway."

I raised an eyebrow at him.

"Of water," he raised his hands with a laugh. "It's just a little warm out here."

Their wedding was being held outdoors under the warmth of the summer sun. While it may be a little warm, it was absolutely beautiful. Like a scene from a fairytale. Outdoor weddings just have a completely different vibe to them.

Ally, smiling, walked behind me, placing her hands over my eyes. Without a word she led me through the sea of chairs. Once we stopped she whispered in my ear. "I have a surprise for you."

Before I could ask what it was, I heard a familiar voice coming from somewhere in front of me.

No, I thought.

It couldn't be.

"I've missed you, man." Fred said, smiling wide as Ally released her hands from over my eyes.

I couldn't believe it. Fred was here, standing directly in front of me.

Tears welled up in my eyes as I pulled my best friend in for a hug.

"I can't believe you're here, man."

Fred leaned back a bit. "I wouldn't miss seeing you in a tux for the world," he laughed. "And you really should thank your girlfriend. She set this all up."

I turned to look at Ally, my heart bursting with love. "You really did this?"

Ally nodded, her own eyes filling up with tears. "I know how much you've been missing home. While I couldn't bring the island to you, I could bring the next best thing," she smiled, gesturing to my best friend.

I gathered her in my arms, kissing her more passionately than ever, not caring who saw.

If I ever had any doubt that this woman was the one for me, this gesture absolutely destroyed it.

The ceremony began, and I could not take my eyes off of my lovely Ally. She was perfect in every way. I'm not sure if I was getting caught up in the romantic atmosphere of today, but I have never felt more in love than I did in this moment.

For the rest of the ceremony, as well as the reception, she was my sole focus. Even while I was seated at a table catching up with Fred, I had my arm around her, not wanting her out of my sight for even a second.

With the love of my life by my side as well as my very best friend, I was sure that life couldn't get any better.

CHAPTER 6

lly

AFTER THE NEWLYWEDS had their first dance as a married couple, the rest of us were invited to join them out on the dance floor.

Darren stood, offering me his hand. With a smile I accepted it, and he led me to the dancefloor. He twirled me around and into his loving arms. He held me close as we swayed to the music.

The night was absolutely perfect, until a tap on Darren's shoulder shattered the moment.

"Damn, you're sexy all dressed up," a female voice said, pulling Darren's attention away from me.

Darren looked at the owner of the voice, and I could feel his body tense up in my arms. "Charlotte," he said through clenched teeth.

I looked between the two of them. I could see Darren's

expression darken. "Charlotte? Who's this?" I asked, not sure if I really wanted to know the answer or not.

"My ex," Darren explained, his confusion mirroring my own.

My heart beat wildly in my chest, so much so that it almost caused physical pain.

I felt sick standing there, as my boyfriend's ex basically undressed him with her eyes. I also wanted to grab her a napkin to mop up all her drool

Darren stood closer to me, placing a protective and reassuring hand on my lower back. "Why are you here Charlotte?"

She cocked her head, looking at him like he had just asked the stupidest question. "To see you, silly. You and I are meant to be together. And I thought that a wedding would be the perfect atmosphere for us to be reunited." She stepped a little closer to him, eyes never leaving him. "Can't you just feel the love?" She asked, almost in a whisper. "You and I . . . we're the real deal. Nothing can stop us."

Charlotte reached out and touched Darren's arm. Even though he acted quickly, ripping his arm out of her grasp, my mind reeled with disbelief. What was happening?

"How did you even find out about this?" Darren gestured to the wedding reception still happening all around us. Anger now radiated off of him in waves.

"I heard Fred on the phone talking about it one day while I was at his restaurant," she shrugged, as if it was no big deal.

"So you just decided . . ."

"That I would surprise you and fly out here," she said, excitement creeping back into her voice. "Isn't it romantic?"

"No," Darren said, and her face fell. "No, it's not romantic. You and I are over. We have been over and I told you we would never be getting back together," he spat, trying to control his anger.

I looked to Charlotte, expecting her to be taken back a little, or at the very least to be looking a little ashamed.

Which she should be.

But she just stood there, unaffected by Darren's anger. She still has the same smile plastered on her face. I began to feel a little sorry for this woman. She was truly delusional.

Trembling from anger, Darren excused himself to the restroom. Fred, who had been watching the exchange from his seat, got up and followed to comfort his best friend.

I watched, feeling helpless as the man I loved seemed to be in pain.

Charlotte, still standing in front of me, suddenly clicked her tongue. I turned to face her, wondering what she could possibly want with me.

Gone was the sweet, innocent look. She now wore a smug smile, her eyes hardening.

"You must be the new girlfriend," she said condescendingly, looking me up and down. Her lip curled in disgust.

If I was anywhere else other than my best friend's wedding, I would smack that look right off her ugly face.

Without warning, she stepped forward, getting directly in my face. "You may be his girlfriend now," she snarled, voice low and slightly intimidating, "but just know that you are only temporary. Darren and I are serious about each other. In fact, we were engaged right before you entered the picture. We were just on a break when you met him, because I had to go away for a while for work. Darren had wanted to stay back on the island."

If possible, she stepped even closer to me. "And now that I'm back, you no longer have a place in Darren's life. So you need to back the hell off." She pointed a finger into my chest, accentuating each word.

I stood there in shock, tears welling up in my eyes. I had so much that I wanted to say to her, to yell at her, put her in her place. But I also didn't want to cry in front of her, to allow myself to look weak in her eyes. I couldn't let her know that her words had gotten to me.

Looking into my eyes, Charlotte smirked with satisfaction. She straightened up, wiping fake dirt off of her dress, then told me, "Just remember, Darren is mine. And you're in the way. I *will* have him back, no matter what." Once she said that she turned on her heels and walked over to the bar.

I remained in the center of the dancefloor, a piece of my heart breaking off with each second that went by.

Stephanie and Lily rushed to my side, asking if I was okay and what happened. I just shook my head. Turning to Lily, I apologized for ruining her wedding, telling her that I needed to go home.

I needed to be alone for a while.

I collapsed on the couch in tears the second I walked through the door.

The day started out so perfect. I was so happy and in love. How did we get here?

How could this have happened?

I've never heard of Charlotte before. Darren had never mentioned her before.

Now I was questioning why that was.

Was she truly crazy? Believing her and Darren were soulmates and that they were going to be together?

Was I really just temporary?

Did Darren still harbor feelings for her? Is that why he hid in the bathroom instead of fully confronting her?

I was so confused.

I was so hurt.

I had so much that I wanted to say to her, but didn't. But then again, it's not my place to. I didn't know her. I wasn't the one who dated her.

I wasn't the one who was possibly still in love with her.

My heart aches.

It was breaking into a million pieces.

After about a half an hour of laying on the couch in tears, I heard the front door open. In walked Darren and Fred. Darren rushed over to me, and the moment I felt his strong arms wrap around me I broke down in a fresh wave of tears.

I love this man. His touch is comforting. But with Charlotte's words bouncing around in my head . . .

I didn't know what to think.

I didn't know what to do.

I hate this.

I hate her.

"Ally, you know we're both here for you," Fred spoke up.

I looked up at him, my eyes now red and puffy. "Thank you," I said, voice barely above a whisper.

Darren held me tighter. "I promise you, nothing Charlotte said was the truth. Everything was a complete and utter lie."

Fred nodded along in agreement. "I can testify to that. That girl is nuts," he laughed.

I was so grateful for these two. But even as they were attempting to cheer me up, I just didn't know what to believe.

I felt so overwhelmed. So confused.

"Thank you, both of you," I told them, slowly breaking out of Darren's grasp to grab a tissue. "I appreciate the two of you trying to help. But I just . . . I think I need some time alone, to think."

Darren's shoulders slumped, his gaze shifting downwards, making me feel horrible. I didn't want to hurt him.

Then he grabbed my hand, giving it a squeeze. "I understand. I'll be here for you whenever you're ready."

"Me too," Fred chimed in. "Come on," he said, slapping

Darren on the shoulder. "You can come crash with me at my hotel."

I could tell Darren was a little reluctant to leave me. But in the end he respected my wishes, leaving me alone with my thoughts.

CHAPTER 7

lly

THE NEXT MORNING I woke up to a text from Fred, asking me if we could meet. I agreed, so when lunchtime rolled around I walked down to the cafe Fred had suggested.

I got there early, sipping on my soda as I waited for their arrival. I drummed my fingers nervously as I continuously scanned the door for them.

Finally, Fred showed up.

Alone.

My heart sank.

I tried not to let it get to me. Maybe Darren was parking the car. Maybe he was just walking slowly.

Maybe . . .

Maybe he had sent Fred here to talk to me alone. To break my heart for him. To tell me that he never wanted to see me again.

I tried to paste on a fake smile as Fred sat down, trying not to show him what I was really feeling.

Fred took a seat across from me. I quickly scanned the door, yet there was still no sign of Darren.

"How are you doing today?" He asked, bringing my attention back to him.

"A little better than yesterday," I lied. Fred smiled. It was genuine and warm. "Where's Darren? I thought he would be coming with you?" I asked hesitantly.

Fred hesitated a moment, his brow furrowing. "He's . . . he's actually with Charlotte at the moment."

The second those words left his mouth I felt my entire world crashing down again.

Fred reached over the table, taking my trembling hand in his. "It's not what you think, I promise," he offered a small smile.

"But why is he with her?" I asked, my voice small. I was on the verge of tears. Hurt and betrayal surged through me, fast and hot.

Fred sat back in his seat. "You heard her at the reception. All those lies she spewed. You should have heard Darren last night. He was so upset. Not only at Charlotte for crashing the wedding, but he was angry at the thought of you getting hurt. He loves you, Ally. He loves you so much that he's sitting down with that witch right now to try and put her in her place."

A small smile played on my lips.

Fred continued. "I've known Darren all my life. That man hasn't been the same since meeting you. I've seen him with other girlfriends. But none have ever come even close to you.

While it hurt thinking of Darren with other women, no matter how irrational, I was a little bit confused by Fred's words. But it was true that he had known Darren all his life and could vouch for his character.

So I decided to just trust what Fred was telling me. Even if it did hurt a little.

No matter what I tried to do to distract myself, my mind kept wandering back to Charlotte and the words she had spoken to me, wondering if there was any grain of truth in anything that she had said.

Fred and I ordered lunch, even though I wasn't feeling the slightest bit hungry. I knew I had to at least eat something though. I hadn't had anything since before the wedding yesterday.

So we sat, chatting and eating while we waited for Darren, who was supposed to meet up with us after he was done speaking with Charlotte.

I began to feel better about everything the more Fred and I talked. He was just this easy going guy. He was also no-nonsense. So I knew he wouldn't lie to me.

Darren was lucky to have him as a friend.

And right now, I felt I was too.

After what felt like an eternity, Darren wandered through the doors of the cafe. Fred excused himself to go have a quick word with him before he got to the table.

"He's all yours," Fred laughed, patting Darren on the back.

"Thanks Fred, for everything," I said, pulling him in for a quick hug.

We decided to go for a walk in the nearby park to talk.

Once we were seated on a bench, Darren let out a huge breath, launching into his explanation.

Charlotte and him had indeed dated, but it was nothing like she had told me.

There was no seriousness.

No engagement.

No promises.

One date.

There was one single date.

Darren and Charlotte had gone to school together, and she had basically obsessed over him all throughout high school. Although, he had not known that fact until years later.

He would see her down at the beach, either lounging around in the sun or hangout at one of his gigs. She would also frequent Fred's restaurant. And with Darren helping out there he ran into her a lot.

So one night, he decided *why the hell not?* And asked her out.

They went to dinner. Everything went great up until the end of the night when she asked him to come home and meet her family.

"Why?" He had asked, thoroughly confused.

"Because you're the one, silly" she exclaimed, as if he should have known. "My parents are going to want to meet the man I'm going to marry."

"Marry?" He asked, eyes wide with shock.

She nodded excitedly.

He told me he had made up some lame excuse and got the hell outta there. But she had refused to give up. Refused to believe that the two of them were not getting married. She ended up pretty much stalking him for months after that.

"Did you ever go to the police?" I asked him.

Darred nodded. "They couldn't do anything though because she hadn't harmed anyone or done anything destructive or violent. There were no threats."

"That's awful." I couldn't imagine having to go through that. "I'm so sorry," I said, leaning onto Darren's shoulder. "And I'm so sorry I ever doubted you, for even a second." A wave of guilt crashed over me.

Darren put his arm around my shoulder. "It's okay," he assured me. "I know firsthand just how persuasive she can be."

EPILOGUE

"So you're sure about this?" Darren asked me once more once we arrived at the airport. "Like, absolutely, one hundred percent sure?"

The three of us - me, Darren, and Fred were back at the airport, a mountain of luggage between us.

After everything that had happened with Charlotte, we sat down and had a heart to heart. Through this we realized that all the two of us need to be happy was each other.

And Fred.

Fred was the friend we all needed.

After this realization we decided that the best thing for us all was to go home.

To the island.

Where we fell in love.

Where our love story began.

Where we belonged.

Besides my friends, there was nothing tying me to the city. And I had to admit, I missed the laid back, slow pace of island life.

It truly felt like home.

I wrapped my arms around Darren's neck, not caring who saw. "I've never been more sure about anything in my life," I assured him. "I love you more than anything. And I'll do anything to be with you. I'll follow you anywhere. Now, let's go home."

The three of us boarded the plane, feeling lighter than we had the last few weeks. We left behind the city lights for the turquoise waters and sandy beaches of our island paradise.

As we spared through the skies towards our new beginning, I felt a sense of peace settle over me at last. I knew there would be challenges ahead, but with Darren by my side, I was ready to face anything.

www.ingramcontent.com/pod-product-compliance
Lightning Source LLC
Chambersburg PA
CBHW061446160726
47995CB00003B/1068